The Gift

OTHER CHRISTMAS BOOKS
BY ANITA STANSFIELD:

A Christmas Melody

A Star in Winter

The Three Gifts of Christmas

The Gift

ANITA STANSFIELD

Covenant Communications, Inc.

Cover art by Jessica A. Warner.
Cover design copyrighted 2005 by Covenant Communications, Inc.

Published by Covenant Communications, Inc.
American Fork, Utah

Copyright © 2005 by Anita Stansfield
All rights reserved. No part of this book may be reproduced in any format or in any medium without the written permission of the publisher, Covenant Communications, Inc., P.O. Box 416, American Fork, UT 84003. This work is not an official publication of The Church of Jesus Christ of Latter-day Saints. The views expressed within this work are the sole responsibility of the author and do not necessarily reflect the position of The Church of Jesus Christ of Latter-day Saints, Covenant Communications, Inc., or any other entity.

This is a work of fiction. The characters, names, incidents, places, and dialogue are products of the author's imagination, and are not to be construed as real.

Printed in Canada
First Printing: October 2005

11 10 09 08 07 06 05   10 9 8 7 6 5 4 3 2 1

ISBN 1-59811-044-6

Los Angeles, California

Brandon Ridge packed some clothes and personal belongings into two pieces of luggage. He wandered through the dumpy apartment, feeling no regret about leaving anything behind. Perhaps if he hadn't needed to sell the piano in order to make ends meet, he might have felt some regret there. But he hadn't been able to play it anyway since the accident, and with the piano gone, there was nothing to keep him here any longer. Briefly closing his eyes, Brandon clearly recalled the moment the car door had slammed on his hand, breaking it in three places. To this day he wasn't sure how it had happened; he only wished he could go back and alter that one moment and the way it had dashed the last bit of hope he'd been clinging to. But now he was leaving here. He opened his eyes to face reality and forced his mind to the present.

The thought of returning home after all these years spontaneously evoked a string of memories that connected this moment to the day he'd left. He honestly couldn't figure how many years it had been. He only knew he'd lived a lifetime here in LA since he'd arrived, barely out of high school, starry-eyed with dreams. He'd come with the belief that his gift of music, this obsession that had been with him from his childhood, would be the means of bringing enormous fame and wealth into his life. He'd come with great dreams of making his family proud, and with the belief that he was strong enough to make it in the dog-eat-dog world of the music industry. And now he was going home—not with fame and glory, but with nothing. Not so many hours ago he'd faced a life-altering choice. He could either take every pill in the house and end it all, or he could call home. He hadn't felt afraid to die; he'd actually been eager to be free of the horrors and heartache of this world. And not having to face his loved ones with the mess he'd made of his life was definitely appealing. But the tiniest glimmer of hope had come with memories of the countless times he'd heard both his father and sister tell him how much they loved him, that they would love him no matter what. So he'd called home instead. And for the first time in years, he'd told them the truth—most of it anyway. They knew he'd been suicidal. They knew his life was a mess, that he had failed utterly and completely. But with any luck, they would never have to know the whole truth.

Waiting for the cab, Brandon began to feel on edge. He told himself he could get through the next hour without taking a pill, but his anxiety became too intense and he had to take one anyway. It was raining when the cab arrived, and he hurried to get his luggage into the trunk. During the drive to the airport he became preoccupied with the rain drizzling down the car windows, and he felt some relief in knowing that he wouldn't ever have to see California rain again—provided his family actually allowed him to stay more than a short while. It wouldn't take his father or Lauren long to figure out the obvious, and then heaven only knew what might happen. A part of him knew it was inevitable that they would discover the truth; he knew at some level that he needed their help, that he couldn't conquer this on his own. But another part of him felt determined to do it alone, to find a way to get himself out of the mess he'd gotten himself into.

Once on the plane, Brandon's dark mood settled in more fully. Waiting for the passengers to board, he again became preoccupied with the rain drizzling down the window. He wondered if it was raining in Utah, and he wondered what it would be like going home. Although he'd kept in touch by telephone with his father and sister, he'd not been home at all for years. Brandon's mother had died in his early childhood, and he and his sister had been raised by their father. Tom Ridge was a good man, and he'd always loved and accepted Brandon, even though Tom's only son had turned his back on the beliefs he'd been raised with, certain it was the only way to follow the music in his heart. Brandon's sister, Lauren, had been married and divorced and had two children he'd never met. Tom had retired and sold his home to move in with Lauren to help her with the kids. And now Brandon was going to stay in the same home somewhere in a new community in Utah Valley that hadn't even existed when he'd left home. And he was going to live with the only family he had, a family that felt like strangers to him. He wondered if it would be Dad or Lauren who would meet him when he got off the plane. And he wondered how he was ever going to get past the mess he'd made of his life. Overcome with a familiar sinking sensation, he got some water from the flight attendant and took a couple of pills. He soon began to relax and was relieved when the flight got underway.

Lauren arrived at the baggage claim area of the airport at exactly the time she knew Brandon's flight was supposed to land. She knew it would take him some time to traverse the long corridors and arrive at where she had to wait, since she wasn't allowed past security. She felt impatient and antsy, glancing at her watch every two minutes, keeping a close eye on the escalators. Brandon had promised their father he would be on that flight, but until she actually saw him, she would keep fearing that he'd regressed in the hours since they'd talked, and maybe he'd done the unthinkable after all. Maybe he'd just told them he would come home to placate them, and was even now seeking out some way of doing away with himself. Or maybe he already had.

Lauren caught her breath when she saw him at the top of the escalator, coming down. Even from this distance she clearly recognized him, in spite of how many years it had been. He wore dark glasses even though he was inside on a cloudy day. He had a bag over one shoulder, and his hair looked a little rumpled. When he stepped off the escalator she saw him hesitate and scan the area until he looked directly at her. For a long moment they just stared at each other from a distance. It was almost like he read her mind when he took off his dark glasses, as if to see her better. They started toward each other in the same moment, and the world seemed to be going in slow motion as she opened her arms and allowed him to fill them. She couldn't hold back tears as she pondered how grateful she was to feel him in her embrace, alive, and breathing, and real. She felt him drop his bag and hug her more tightly, as if they shared the same emotion without exchanging a word. He finally drew back and looked at her tears with a furrowed brow.

"No need for this," Brandon said, wiping them away. He could never tell her what her love and acceptance meant to him.

"It's been so long," she said. "I'm just so grateful . . . that you're here . . . and you're all right."

"All right is relative," he said. "But I'm grateful to be here as well."

After his other bag appeared on the rotating luggage carousel, Lauren picked up the one he'd left sitting at his feet. "I can get it," he said.

"So can I," she said. "This way you can hold my hand."

She took his left hand in hers, then looked down at it in surprise. There was something stiff and unnatural in the way he threaded his fingers between hers, as if it took conscious effort. He apparently noticed her attention to it and said, "Yes, it's deformed."

"Does it still hurt?" she asked.

"Only if I try to do something that takes any effort—like opening a can or something."

She made no further comment about his hand, and he was grateful. Through his somewhat regular phone calls, she was well aware of the freak accident that had injured his hand, and the surgery that had followed. What she didn't know was how it had been the final straw. Throughout all the tough and disappointing years in LA, his ability to make music—if only for his own ears—had kept him grounded and centered. Then, with his left hand useless, the painkillers he'd been given following the surgery had quickly become his only method of being able to cope with his failed goals and broken dreams.

They said nothing as they walked to the car, except for Brandon's comment, "It's cold here."

"It's a beautiful fall day," she said. "Well, a little cloudy, but a nice day."

They loaded the luggage into her car, and within minutes they were on the freeway.

It was dark before they finally headed into Lauren's neighborhood. Brandon's thoughts wandered as he gazed absently out the window. The vague sense of detachment from his surroundings felt familiar, as did the underlying fear that knotted his stomach. But he couldn't deny feeling some measure of comfort in being with Lauren. Her presence soothed something in him. She didn't have to say anything for him to know that she loved and accepted him.

As Lauren pulled into the driveway of her home, it felt vaguely familiar, if only from pictures he'd seen. They pulled into the garage, and Brandon barely had his door open before Tom appeared in the doorway to the house. Without a word he wrapped Brandon in his fatherly embrace, and they held each other for a long moment. Then

Tom took Brandon's face into his hands. "I'm grateful to see you alive and well, son," he said.

"I'm grateful to be here," Brandon said.

Tom helped carry Brandon's luggage into the house. Brandon noticed the home was beautifully decorated, and it had a cozy warmth to it that he'd somehow expected. He and his dad followed Lauren up the stairs and in through the first door on the right. As Tom set down the bag he was carrying, Lauren said, "The closet and drawers are empty. Feel free to move in and make yourself at home. If you need something, you'll have to speak up and let one of us know." She motioned with her hand toward a door. "This room has its own bathroom, so you can have your space and privacy."

"Thank you," Brandon said, trying to be gracious and not let on how tense and agitated he felt.

"I'll have supper ready in about ten minutes," Tom said, putting a hand on Brandon's shoulder. "We'll see you downstairs."

"Thank you," he said again and watched them leave the room. With the door closed he hurried to find a couple of pills to take, knowing he'd never get through the evening without them.

Lauren was urging the kids to the table when Brandon entered the dining room. Seeing him in good light without his dark glasses, she noticed his eyes looked tired and strained. She introduced him to the children, and he politely acknowledged them.

Lauren noticed that as the meal began, Brandon seemed depressed and exhausted, and she felt deeply concerned for him. But by the time they were finished, he'd perked up considerably and was even joking with their father, almost like his old self. He insisted on helping with the dishes and seemed to have found a second wind.

Brandon sat to visit a bit with his father while Lauren helped her kids with their homework. But the conversation felt tense and strained. He finally pleaded exhaustion and said goodnight. He found Lauren in the kitchen and told her goodnight as well.

"Do you have everything you need?" she asked.

"I do, thank you," he said.

"It's good to have you here, Brandon. I feel a little less worried about you, knowing you're here with us."

"Well, it's nice to know somebody cares," he said and went to his room and straight to bed. With the right amount of medication he slept deep and long. He woke up with a headache, took a couple of pills, and got in the shower. With hot water running over his face, he thought of the circumstances of his life, and an unexpected spurt of emotion rushed out of him. He leaned his head against the side of the shower and cried until he could manage to stuff the pain back where it belonged. He dried off and took a couple more pills before he got dressed and ventured through the house in search of life. He found Lauren typing at a computer just off of the kitchen; he knew that she had some kind of job she did at home. She greeted him warmly and told him that their father had gone out to brunch with an old friend, and that the kids were at school.

Lauren stopped typing and looked up at him, taking note of the dark glasses he wore. "It's cloudy, you know," she said, "not to mention we're in the house. They call those *sunglasses* because most people wear them in the sun."

"The light hurts my eyes," he said. "Cloudy or not."

"And why is that?"

"I have a headache," he said.

"Do you get headaches often?"

"Yes, actually," he said and was relieved that she didn't press him further on that.

"Are you hungry?" she asked, coming to her feet.

"Not really."

"Well, you need to eat something."

"A piece of toast would be fine, and I'm certain I can get that myself by nosing around in the kitchen a little."

"You probably could," she said, "but I can show you around in the kitchen a little until you get used to it." Brandon watched her pour him some orange juice and make a couple of pieces of toast. He was hating the silence between them until she broke it by saying, "What's going on?"

"What do you mean?"

"I mean," she said, giving him a hard stare, "that you told me on the phone you were seriously considering taking your own life, Brandon, and I'm still having trouble coming to terms with that." She started to cry. "I don't understand. Help me understand why you would do that so I can stop fearing that you'll consider it again."

Brandon sighed loudly and looked away. The reasons were complicated, and some of them he simply wasn't ready to talk about. But it wasn't difficult for him to admit his most prominent thought.

"And why should I want to live when I am a failure at everything I have done in my life, everything that mattered to me at all?"

"Failure? Is that what you said? *Failure?*"

"That's right." He sounded insulted by her astonishment, as if she should agree completely.

"A failure? You've got to be kidding me." Lauren made a noise of disbelief. "Where is this coming from, Brandon?"

"It's a fact, Lauren. Why is that so difficult to see? Do I have to spell it out for you?"

"I guess you do, because I *can't* see it."

He leaned forward, his countenance angry. "Fine," he said. "I'm a musician, Lauren. It's been a part of me for as long as I can remember. That's it; that's all I am, and I failed."

"Are you trying to tell me your value as a human being is based on your ability to what . . . sell records?" He didn't answer, and she went on. "I understand your gift is a great part of you, but that's not who you are, Brandon. There are countless ways to find fulfillment and bless lives with your gift. You still have so much life to live, so much to offer. The value of a gift is not measured by its ability to produce the dollar. And your value as a person has nothing to do with your ability to do anything. You have value just by being you."

Brandon took a deep breath as if he could literally soothe his soul with her words. "Where do you come up with this stuff?" he asked.

"I just say exactly what I feel needs to be said."

"You do it well, I must admit. And you've given me something to think about."

Over the next few days, Brandon tried to integrate himself into the family's schedule, but he felt out of sorts and uncomfortable. Lauren kept busy with her children, her typing, and a Church calling. Dad helped with the kids and some of the cooking and played golf nearly every day. He invited Brandon to go along, but he simply wasn't interested.

There was a familiarity to Lauren's home that he couldn't quite pinpoint. He suspected it had something to do with the presence of certain things that he'd not been exposed to for years. On the walls there were pictures of Christ, and temples, and even the current prophet; Brandon didn't know his name. He'd been raised with the gospel being the central focus of life. In his heart he believed that Christ was real, and that the basis of all he'd been taught was true.

He'd just never felt it was important enough to put the same effort into it that he'd seen so many other people do. While he paid little attention to the abundant decor that made it evident he was staying in a Christian home, he couldn't deny feeling drawn to a large print of Christ in the front room. It hung above the piano. But since being anywhere near the piano made him highly uncomfortable, he avoided that room altogether.

Lauren discreetly observed her brother as he settled in. She wondered what it was about his behavior that made her uneasy. It had been years since they'd lived under the same roof, but still, she knew something wasn't right. There were moments when he seemed almost like himself. At times he talked and laughed with her or their father, as if nothing in the world was wrong. He interacted some with the children, and occasionally the dog. But more often than not, he was subtly irritable and easily provoked. He slept late in the morning, went to bed early in the evenings, and he took long naps. Sometimes he was shaky, almost despondent, and at other times he was full of energy. And he often wore those dark glasses, claiming that he had a headache and that even the lights in the house hurt his eyes. She came right out and asked him if he was doing drugs; he swore to her that he'd never taken any drug that hadn't come from a pharmacy. Lauren sincerely tried to accept Brandon's explanation for his behavior, but she felt deeply uneasy nonetheless. She knew something wasn't right, and she wanted to be able to help him, but the answers eluded her.

Following a twenty-four-hour fast on his behalf, and a great deal of fervent prayer, Lauren woke up in the middle of the night with a mild headache and opened the medicine chest in search of some Tylenol. Moving bottles around, she noticed an old prescription with her ex-husband's name on it and was surprised. She thought she'd gotten rid of all those. It was a generic painkiller he'd been given when he'd had some oral surgery done a month or so before the divorce. He'd only taken three or four of the original thirty pills. She set it out on the counter to remind herself to flush the pills down the toilet in the morning. She went back to bed and noticed the bottle there the next morning when she was brushing her teeth, but she'd gotten up late and had to hurry to get the kids off to school. It was after lunch before she went back to the bathroom to put some clean towels away. She saw the bottle sitting there and took off the lid to dump the pills down the toilet. She looked inside and asked herself if she were going crazy. Had she not seen this bottle nearly full in the middle of the night? And now there were only two pills left in the bottom. And then it hit her like a bolt of lightning. She went upstairs to Brandon's room, knowing that he was in the basement with their father. She pulled open the dresser drawers and found some of them completely empty. Rummaging haphazardly through the ones that held his clothes and personal items, she was not surprised to see a prescription bottle, then another, and another. She set them on top of the dresser and kept looking. Twelve, thirteen, fourteen. She lined the bottles up. Some were empty; most had at least a few pills in them. She looked at the labels. Different drugs. Different pharmacies. Different doctors. She felt sick to her stomach and started to cry. She opened the closet and checked the pockets of his clothes. She found two more bottles and some loose pills. She looked in his luggage in the bottom of the closet and found nine more bottles. She sobbed as she pulled them into her hands. She couldn't believe it. *She couldn't believe it!*

Brandon heard a strange sound as he approached the door to his room. He stepped in and his heart dropped to see Lauren kneeling on the floor by the open closet door, pill bottles in each hand—crying. He glanced at the dresser where the drawers were open and several bottles were lined up. He'd been busted. His first impulse was to get angry and tell her to mind her own business. But he knew he'd only be making a fool of himself. In his heart he knew he needed her help, and he couldn't go on pretending. At some level this was what he'd been hoping for when he'd found the bottle of Hydrocodone on the bathroom counter this morning. He'd secretly wanted her to notice the pills missing, which would prevent him from mustering the courage to tell her the truth spontaneously. Brandon forced a calm voice and asked, "What are you doing?"

Lauren turned to look at him and shot to her feet. "How many are there, Brandon?" she shouted. "How many different drugs?" He didn't answer, and she shouted louder. "How many different pharmacies? How many different doctors have you been seeing?" He said nothing, and she screamed, "You stole drugs from me! I can't believe this!" She set the bottles in her hands down with the others.

"I have trouble believing it myself," Brandon said, then Tom appeared in the doorway, looking concerned.

"Why all the shouting?" he demanded.

"You tell him!" Lauren said to Brandon. "It's time you owned up."

"Yes, it is," Brandon said, his voice barely steady. Tears came to his eyes, and he could barely speak enough to say, "Just . . . give me a minute."

Tom sat beside him on the bed and put a hand on his shoulder. While Brandon was trying to control his emotions, their father looked up at Lauren in question. She glanced toward the top of the dresser. Tom's eyes followed, then widened in horror. But neither of them said anything. Lauren felt certain their father knew, just as she knew, that Brandon needed to admit to the problem himself.

"Talk to me, son," Tom said gently.

"Uh . . . I um . . ." He pushed his hands brutally through his hair and tugged at it, groaning. He swallowed carefully and tried again. "I . . ." He groaned again.

"Is it so hard to say?" Lauren asked.

"Yes!" he snapped and looked up at her. "Yes, it's hard to say, alright?" He shot to his feet and began to pace. "Maybe if I could have said it a long time ago, I could have told you over the phone and it wouldn't have gotten this bad. How can I say it when I have trouble even believing that it's come to this? How can I accept that . . ." His voice broke again. He looked at Lauren, then his father. "I . . . have a drug problem." He raised a trembling hand and wiped it over his face. "I have a serious drug problem."

Tom said gently, "Then we need to do whatever it takes to solve the problem."

Brandon tried to chuckle, but it came out as a sob. He hurried to say, "I thought I could beat it. I thought I could . . . have the discipline to just . . . stop. But I can't."

"You can't just stop taking stuff like this," Lauren said. "The withdrawal from some of these could kill you."

"How do you know that?" he growled.

"I catch an episode of *Oprah* once in a while. But it doesn't take a rocket scientist to figure that the combination of this many drugs has got to be close to lethal. How are you even alive?"

"There are only four different drugs there, Lauren. Some of them are different brand names for the same drug."

"And how did you get all of this?" she asked.

Brandon shook his head and sat back down; his father's arm went around his shoulders. "I don't think I should admit to that."

"Why not?" Lauren demanded.

"Because it wasn't necessarily legal."

"Oh, good heavens," Lauren muttered and moved toward the door.

"Where are you going?" Brandon demanded.

"I'm going to make some calls. I'm hoping we can come up with enough money to pay for a decent rehab program."

Brandon just nodded and watched her walk away. Then he cried. He cried like he hadn't cried since he'd lost the use of his hand. And his father just gave him the shoulder to cry against.

Nearly two hours later, Brandon was all but asleep on his bed with his dad sitting in a chair nearby. Lauren walked into the room and said, "Okay, here's the deal. Are you awake, Brandon? You need to hear this."

"I'm awake," he said, but he remained lying down. His head was killing him.

"God is smiling upon us," she said, but she still sounded upset. "There is a decent rehabilitation center less than an hour from here. This place actually has specialists who focus on prescription-drug addiction. They'll work with us on the finances, and they have a couple of spaces open. We will be taking you there in the morning. You and your luggage will be searched for drugs of any kind, and you will not be popping another pill once you walk in the door, except for the medication you will be given under *one* doctor's supervision to help temper the withdrawal."

Brandon squeezed his eyes closed and groaned. "Is there anything else I need to know before I sentence myself to this . . . prison?" he asked.

"They said the fact that you're willing to get help is a huge step ahead of most people they have to deal with; many of them are there on court orders."

"Oh, I'll give myself a pat on the back for that," Brandon said with sarcasm.

Through the remainder of the day Brandon took the usual pills without feeling guilty. His family knew he was taking them, if only to cope until he crossed the bridge into a drug-free world in the morning. He didn't have to worry about running out. He didn't have to wonder what he was going to do about this problem. But he felt scared out of his mind.

Late that evening Lauren found him in his room. He was surprised when she asked, "Why is it that you've been here for days and you've not once touched the piano?"

Since Lauren knew he had a drug problem, he didn't figure there was any point in avoiding the truth about everything else. He admitted with a heavy voice, "I haven't touched it since the surgery, other than the one time I tried to do something with my right hand and it just didn't work."

He was surprised when she took his left hand into hers. "How bad is it?" she asked, and he slowly opened and closed his fingers, demonstrating their limited range of motion. "Where does it hurt?" she asked, rubbing the muscles of his hand. He flinched a couple of times, and it was easy for her to tell where without him saying anything. "Have you been doing physical therapy?"

"Not lately," he said, and she gave him a sharp glare.

"Why not?"

"What's the point? The music is all dried up inside of me."

"Surely that's temporary," she said. "But either way, you need to do the exercises so you can regain the use of your hand. Whether you play music or not, you need your hand. Isn't it difficult to do a lot of things?"

"I manage," was all he said. He didn't want to admit to her what he could barely admit to himself—that he was using the pain and weakness in his hand as an excuse to hide from the music.

"Well, you need to do the therapy," she said, continuing to rub his hand. "You never know when your gift might return, and you'll wish you had your hand."

"It's a thing of the past, Lauren. It's over."

"I don't believe that," she said, but she sounded angry. Was she angry with him? Or angry with what he'd made of his life? Her voice softened as she added, "Your gift is still in there somewhere, and it's incredible. Do you have any idea how amazing you are? Even in high school, I was so in awe of your talent."

"That's in the past," he said, but she just shook her head. He appreciated her efforts, and her belief in him, but he wasn't certain he could ever believe in himself enough to bring his gift back to life.

The following morning Brandon felt completely dehumanized as the rehab attendants searched both him and his luggage. Even as humiliating as it was, he was grateful to have his dad and Lauren with him through the ridiculous amount of paperwork and harsh debriefing about the rules. It was made plainly evident that Brandon was giving up his will and his freedom to these people, and no matter how much he hated it, he would be governed by them until he became capable of governing his own life. When it came time for his dad and Lauren to leave, Brandon was reminded of the moment he'd realized his mother would die. He'd felt like a lost child, alone and terrified. He hugged them each tightly, trying to pull their love into himself. As Lauren held to him tightly, she whispered near his ear, "I will be praying for you constantly. God will get you through this, Brandon. Nobody else can. He will give you the peace and the strength you need." She looked into his eyes with tears in her own. "Remember that."

Brandon nodded but couldn't speak. He was determined to maintain his dignity, but he was barely holding onto it. Fearing a complete breakdown, he forced himself to step back, then he turned and walked away, feeling as if he were about to literally descend into the depths of hell. And nobody could spare him from the inevitable consequences of the choices he'd made to bring his life to this point. Not even God could do that.

Lauren kept her promise to pray for her brother constantly. He was in her thoughts and in her heart every minute of every day. They'd not been close for many years, but she felt a deep affinity with him that she could never put in words. He was her brother, and he needed her. When the day came that they could finally see Brandon, knowing that the detoxification process was over, Lauren felt almost as terrified as she had the day they'd taken him in, a week earlier. Her concern deepened when her father came down with the flu and was too ill to go with her. Going into the facility, she underwent a search similar to the one Brandon had endured in order to make certain she wasn't smuggling anything in that might set him back. She was then taken down a long hall to his room. She held her breath as she entered the room and found him sitting on the floor, leaning against the bed, his head down. He wore jeans and a button-up shirt that was only partially buttoned. His feet were bare. He was nervously rubbing his left hand with the fingers of his right, as if to rub out the pain and stiffness that she knew was there.

"You have company," the attendant said, and Brandon's head shot up. Lauren couldn't keep from gasping. He looked more ill than her father, who had been vomiting all night. His eyes looked sunken, his skin sallow. He looked thinner, more fragile. He looked broken.

"Thank you," Brandon said, his voice weak. The attendant left the room, leaving the door open.

Lauren watched Brandon take hold of the edge of the bed and come unsteadily to his feet. She rushed toward him and took hold of his arm to help him, immediately wrapping him in her arms.

"Oh, Lauren," he muttered near her ear, holding her tightly against him.

She took his face into her hands and pressed her brow to his, just as she'd done the night before he'd come here. "Are you okay?" she asked.

"Better now . . . that you're here." He teetered slightly, and she urged him to the edge of the bed, sitting beside him. "Sorry," he said. "I haven't been able to eat much, but that's getting better."

They sat down on the bed, and he folded one leg underneath him and turned to face her fully, taking both her hands into his. Lauren looked into his strained and weary eyes. She said intently, "What can I do to help you through this?"

"Just be with me," he said, putting his head in her lap. "I don't know how long they'll let you stay, but . . . just be with me." Brandon closed his eyes and became hypnotized by the feel of her fingers brushing his hair back from his face. It reminded him vaguely of his mother. She began to hum, and the music had a soothing effect on Brandon. He muttered quietly, "Sing me that song."

"What song?"

"You used to sing it to me when we were kids . . . after Mom died . . . whenever I was scared."

Lauren cleared her throat and sang through all the verses of "I Am a Child of God" five times. When she tried to quit, he begged her not to. She did variations on the melody for variety, and finally said, "How about a different song?"

"Okay," he said, but before she could think of one he asked, "Do you really believe that's true?"

"What?"

"That we really are children of God?"

"Absolutely. And God loves His children, not collectively, but individually. Think of the love Dad has for us, no matter what we do. That's how God loves you, only more so."

Brandon looked up at her in surprise. "How can He love me when I've been such an idiot?"

"God's love is not conditional on our behavior. It's perfect, constant, absolute. Does Dad love you any less because you made some mistakes?"

"He doesn't seem to, which is something that's always amazed me."

"So, if we as imperfect human beings love our children that much, why is it so difficult to imagine that a perfect God, who is the father of our spirits, would love us any less?"

"I never thought of it that way," he said. "And you really think it's true? Does He really exist? Does He care? Because if He doesn't, I don't see any point in even going through this."

"I know it's true, Brandon," she said, and then she sang, "'Heavenly Father, are you really there? And do you hear and answer every child's prayer?'"

Brandon listened to her sing that song three times, marveling at the tangible warmth that filled him. Perhaps it was true. Perhaps God *did* love him. And if that was true, maybe he could get through this after all.

The following day Brandon began a rigorous schedule that included intense counseling sessions now that he'd completed the horrendous experience of detoxification. He quickly realized that he would never get out of this place if he didn't stick to the program. A part of him felt tempted to just give these people the answers they wanted, if only to convince them that he was fine now. But something deeply instinctive told him that he needed to truly cleanse himself of the underlying pain that had lured him into drug abuse. He didn't just want to get out of here, he wanted to be healthy and strong. He wanted to be happy.

The difficulty came when he began to realize the width of the chasm between his present state and his goal. His personal counselor, a woman named Venice, told him he was a relatively emotionally healthy person who simply had some unresolved issues. She felt confident that his road to dealing with those issues was not necessarily long or complicated, but it could be intense and difficult. After a few sessions together, she committed to spending more time with him than the usual two or three hours a week, if only to get him past the initial strain of what he had to face.

He was glad to see Dad and Lauren on the weekend, but he felt shaky and tense and knew they couldn't help but notice. He couldn't admit to them that while he was grateful to be without the drugs, he ached for the euphoria they had given him. He hungered for the numbness that had protected him from the pain that festered inside of him.

The days dragged on while he relived the grief of losing his mother and the many poor choices he'd made in the years since, apparently in some feeble attempt to compensate for that loss. He ached and struggled to find some measure of peace over the grief he'd endured—and the grief he'd created for others—but it continued to elude him. He had come to terms with the fact that he'd used his gift of music to soothe his way through the hurts of his life, and when he was no longer able to play the piano, he'd unconsciously turned to the drugs as a substitute.

While he felt himself being emotionally dissected, Brandon sank to a state that felt even more horrific than the detoxifying process. He felt utterly and completely broken, and he wished many times that he had just chosen suicide when he'd had the nerve.

Brandon was dismayed to learn that Venice wanted to bring his father and sister in to share in some counseling sessions. She spouted statistics about how much more likely he was to stay away from the drugs if he had the support of his family. But the very idea made him sick to his stomach.

Once their first session together got underway, he tried to be grateful for their love and support and not think too hard about what he was putting them through. When asked how he felt his family was involved in the problem, he resisted the urge to shout at Venice and simply said, "This is my problem. How I chose to respond to every situation in my life is my responsibility. Their being here is simply for the purpose of . . . helping me come to terms with everything that's happened, so I can . . . go on."

"That was a very healthy, appropriate thing to say, Brandon," Venice said, and Brandon shot out of his chair.

"Well it doesn't *feel* healthy! It feels *pathetic,* and I *hate* it! Why do they even have to be a part of this? They have done nothing but love me and care for me, and what have I given them except grief?" He kicked the chair he'd been sitting on, and it slid across the floor. "This has nothing to do with them!" he shouted.

"It most certainly does," Tom said, apparently unaffected by Brandon's anger—unlike Lauren, who was crying. "We're family, Brandon."

He stood and took hold of Brandon's shoulders with a vehemence that was startling. He met him eye-to-eye, saying in a harsh whisper, "The choices you made *are* your responsibility, Brandon. But there is nothing you can do or say that will ever make me stop loving you." He clenched his teeth and actually sounded angry as he added, "I know you're hurting, and I know you're angry, and you have a right to be. I lost her too, but I'm not going to lose you. Families stick together no matter what; families carry each other through the bad times as well as the good. Families are forever, Brandon." As if to emphasize his words, Tom put his arms around Brandon and held him tightly. Brandon felt hesitant to return the embrace, as if he were somehow unworthy of the incredible love his father was so willing to give him. He finally felt himself relax and lifted his arms to more fully accept the expression of fatherly love he was being given. The anger dissolved into a harsh, raw sorrow. Brandon pressed his face to his father's shoulder and wept.

The following week, after struggling through many more days of intense therapy and grueling emotion, Lauren came alone to see Brandon.

"I can't stay long," she said, "but there's something I have to say."

"Okay," he said, facing her directly. "I know we made a deal years ago not to talk about religion, but if I don't say the words that have been rolling in my head for days, I will never be able to live with myself."

"I'm listening," he said when she hesitated.

Lauren visibly summoned her courage, and he realized how his rebellion must have hurt her in years past. "You were raised with the gospel, Brandon. I know that somewhere deep down you believe in Christ, that you call yourself a Christian. But if you really understood what Christ did, you would realize that the real gift He gave can get you through this. You claim to be a Christian, but do you really know what that means? As I see it, being a Christian is not just a matter of believing in what Christ did, but accepting it into our lives and making it a part of who and what we are. He paid the price, Brandon—not only for our sins, our mistakes, our weaknesses—but for our sorrow, our grief, our *pain*. There comes a point where we don't have to carry those burdens if we will only give them to Him. He already endured the pain—all of it. I know it, Brandon. I know it's true beyond any shadow of a doubt." Her voice broke, and tears welled in her eyes. "In a way I'm only beginning to understand it myself; I have a long way to go. But I have felt the peace in my heart, Brandon. I have struggled myself to come to terms with losing Mom, and I've struggled with the reasons my marriage fell apart when I tried so hard to do what's right. But through it all I have felt an underlying peace that no words can describe. And my pain is tempered by perfect peace. You can have that peace too, Brandon. It's there for the asking. That's the only way you can ever fully heal."

"For the asking," he repeated, only slightly cynical.

"That's right," she said. "It's called the Atonement, Brandon, and it's—"

"I know what it's called," he said. "But you're right; I probably have no idea what it means. I believe God's hand has been in my life; I've had miracles. But being free of this pain just seems too impossible to believe. It's too real, too intense. Maybe I just have to accept that it's part of who and what I am, and I just have to learn to live with it."

"And maybe you don't," she said, putting her hands over his shoulders. "Just break the word down. At-one-ment. When you can be at one with God, you will find the peace you're seeking. And remember, I will always be praying for you."

Two days later, Venice ended a session with Brandon by saying, "Would you like to go home for Thanksgiving?"

"You mean I'm done?" he asked.

"No, but you can go home for a few hours for Thanksgiving dinner—if you want to. I think you can handle it. You've gotten past the anger."

"Now I'm just depressed," he admitted, not bothering to point out any of the other obvious facts. He was still shaky sometimes, and he felt a longing for what he knew the drugs could do for him. He hadn't adjusted to the lingering pain inside of him that ached to be medicated.

"So, a visit home couldn't hurt in that regard, could it? What do you think?"

Brandon was surprised to realize that it was a difficult decision. He felt almost afraid to leave this place. As much as he hated it, he'd developed a comfortable routine where he didn't have to make any big decisions, and his boundaries were very clear. The day before Thanksgiving, he became distracted during a group session as he watched snow fall outside the window. He'd not seen snow since he'd left home years ago. And it was beautiful. When the session was over, he stood at the window for a few minutes, noting the equalizing effect the snow had. Everything was white. Everything looked the same. It was beautiful. In that moment he realized that he really wanted to go home for Thanksgiving.

Little was said the following day during the drive to Lauren's home, but Brandon didn't feel uncomfortable with his father. The sun shone from a gleaming blue sky, illuminating yesterday's snowfall with brilliance. The mountains to the east were breathtaking. He had certainly noticed them since his return, but with his mind cleared, they stood out even more prominently.

Brandon felt poignantly reminded of his youth when he walked into the house and the smells of Thanksgiving dinner struck his senses. Lauren met him with a hug, then told him to relax until they were ready to eat. He wandered into the front room and stood beside the piano. He stared at the keys with a deep longing, but he couldn't bring himself to touch them. When he knew that his left hand would refuse to respond the way he wanted it to, trying to play only depressed him. Where music had once eased his pain, now the pain he carried had become such a vivid part of him that he feared it would only contaminate the music—even if he could play. His eyes were drawn upward to the painting of Christ. Brandon stared at it for several minutes, contemplating the piercing blue eyes looking back at him. His mind recounted the things Lauren had told him about the Atonement, and he wondered if they were true. Did such a miracle truly exist for *him* with all his weakness and shortcomings? Was it truly possible to be free of the pain he carried inside of him? Desperately longing for that release, he figured it couldn't hurt to try. *It's there for the asking,* Lauren had said. But it couldn't be that easy. Surely it would take time—and faith. The question, then, was if he could come up with enough faith.

In a whisper he heard himself say, "Are you really there? Is it really true? If so, I beg you to take this pain from me. Help me to go on, help me understand."

Brandon heard the call from the other room that dinner was ready. He looked up once more into the eyes of the Savior, praying in his heart that he could be among the saved.

* ❋ *

Thanksgiving dinner tasted so good to Brandon that he realized how bad the food was at the rehab center. Not horrible, but certainly not like this. He told Lauren three times what an amazing cook she was, then he insisted on helping wash the dishes.

When that was done, they found Dad and the kids digging out the Christmas lights. Brandon spent the next hour on the roof helping his father put them up, then he had some pie before it was time to go back.

Lauren drove him back to the city while Dad stayed with the children. Following many miles of silence, she said, "You will be spending Christmas with us, won't you?"

"I don't know. I hadn't thought about it. Maybe I'll still be in prison."

"I don't think so," she said. "Venice gave me the impression it wouldn't be too much longer." She turned to look at him for a long moment, then focused back on the road. "We really would like you to stay for Christmas. You can stay indefinitely, if you like." He liked that idea, but he didn't know what to say. He was relieved when she went on. "Venice said it would be good for you not to be alone until you adjust more fully. And you'll be doing some outpatient counseling for a while. So, you'll just *have* to stay through the holidays at least."

"I suppose I will," he said. "Thank you."

Returning to the facility was even more difficult for Brandon than he'd anticipated, but spending time at home had made a remarkable change in him. He wanted to get out of here. He wanted to put this behind him and not only be with his family for Christmas, but for all of the holiday preparations that he'd gotten a little taste of in putting up the lights. Christmas had been so meaningless in the years since he'd gone to LA. The idea of sharing the holiday with these people he loved was terribly inviting.

The following day, Venice gave Brandon a projected release date of December eleventh. She told him he was doing well, and barring any setbacks, she felt confident that he would be ready to make it on his own and stay drug free. Brandon appreciated her faith in him, and for the most part he agreed with her. But he continued to be plagued with a hovering pain that seemed to be a conglomeration of each of the losses he'd endured in his life. He couldn't even think about certain things without being tormented with uncomfortable thoughts and feelings. He wanted them to go away, mostly because at some level they frightened him.

A week before his release date, Venice told him that she'd talked to Lauren and had arranged for him to have another outing. Brandon felt as excited as a child as he anticipated the day she was coming to pick him up. He had no idea what her plans were; he didn't care. He was going to be out of this place for a number of hours. And this excursion marked one week until he would be released. The reality of having such an enormous milestone behind him filled him with real hope. If only he could be free of the pain!

Brandon couldn't hold back a little laugh when he saw Lauren. In the car he asked, "Where are we going?"

"Well, I thought it might be better to stay close and not waste precious time on the road."

They drove into the heart of Salt Lake City, past places that had once been so familiar to him. She parked at one of the downtown malls where they had some lunch, then they wandered through the Joseph Smith Memorial building, and outside they wandered through some beautiful grounds east of the temple that hadn't been there the last time he'd come to this place. They stood by a little pool and looked up at the magnificent temple edifice. They moved farther north and entered Temple Square through the north gate, then they went into the North Visitors' Center. Brandon only had vague memories of coming here once, but it had been so long ago that he had no idea what Lauren's purpose might be. She seemed to be headed somewhere specific as she took his hand and led him past some paintings and displays, paying them no mind. They started walking up a wide circular ramp, then all of a sudden it came into view. Brandon slowed his pace as his focus lifted to the huge, magnificent statue of Christ, His arms outstretched. He wondered how he could have forgotten that this was here.

"It's incredible," he murmured as they moved to stand directly facing the statue.

"I thought you might like to see it again."

"Oh yes," he said distantly. He was more preoccupied with the way standing there made him feel.

Lauren watched Brandon's expression as he took in the glory of the *Christus*. He looked like a child seeing snow for the first time, his eyes wide, full of innocence and awe. The visible effect was so touching that she felt near tears. She prayed in her heart that he would be even more affected within, that he would be able to come to understand and accept the miracle of all that Christ stood for, and to allow its healing power to purge his battered spirit.

Brandon felt reluctant to go and was relieved when Lauren guided him to a bench where she seemed content to just sit with her hand in his, gazing upward with him while he pondered all he was feeling. People came and went, some posing for pictures, some just gazing. And most of them seemed so happy.

As Brandon pondered the state of his life, he ached to be free of the pain that plagued him. Without hardly thinking about it, he looked up at the statue and prayed silently with all the energy of his soul, *Please give me peace, Lord. I'll do anything you ask of me, just free me from this pain.*

While they sat in silence for several minutes longer, the thought occurred to him that, for the moment, the best thing he could do for God—and himself—was to get through rehab and stop being a burden to the people around him.

They finally stood up, took another long look at the statue, then started down the ramp. They moved slowly past some of the displays in the downstairs lobby, then back outside. It was dark now, and they moved through the square, which was lit up for Christmas with thousands of little colored lights. He felt like a child again, surrounded by something magical and warm that he couldn't describe but longed to hold onto.

Brandon hated going back to the center, but he fought to hold with him the glimmer of peace he'd felt while contemplating the image of Christ. Throughout the next day he felt as if he were in some kind of fog, as if he was perhaps supposed to understand something he *didn't* understand. He went to dinner as usual, but as he moved across the room to sit down, his eye was drawn to something he'd seen there every day since he'd first come, but he'd given it no attention; he'd not wanted anything to do with it. But now the little spinet piano called to him. While he ate, he couldn't keep his eyes off of it. He knew he could do very little with his left hand, but suddenly that felt like a challenge rather than a detriment.

Sizing up the situation, he realized he was kept far too busy to have time to play the piano in the midst of all the other things that he was required to do and attend. He concluded that the best time to do it would be in the night, when everyone else was asleep. And fortunately, this room was a significant distance from the dorms where everyone slept. There were people on night duty, but since he was well-known as a non-troublemaker, he figured he could win them over.

Brandon went to bed thinking about the piano, then his mind drifted to the image of Christ he had seen at Temple Square. The peace he'd felt then came back to him, and he quickly fell asleep. He woke up in the dark, realizing his plan to stay awake and play the piano had been foiled by falling asleep. He glanced at the clock. Four forty-two. He still had time. He hurried to get dressed and went quietly through the halls to the room of his destination. He flipped on the light and moved stealthily toward the instrument with a kind of reverence. "Hello, my friend," he said, lifting the cover off of the keys. He sat on the bench and felt his heart quicken with a combination of fear and excitement. He concentrated on the song he'd been hearing in his head, something that had germinated while he was at Temple Square listening to Christmas music. With his right hand he quickly picked out the melody, hearing himself laugh as he heard music come through his fingers. He worked out a variety of embellishments on the melody, and, without even thinking, he lifted his left hand onto the keys to play. He stopped abruptly when it wouldn't respond the way his mind told it to. Then the thought occurred to him that all he really needed to give the song some depth was to add a very simple bass line. Surely he could get his fingers—as stiff as they were—to play a two-note sequence over and over. He tried it. It worked. He laughed and kept working at it for a few minutes until it was coming naturally, fluidly. Then he put his right hand into the mix, and music filled the room, but more importantly it filled his soul. He went through the song three or four times, finding a pattern to his rendition of "O Little Town of Bethlehem." He heard himself singing spontaneously. The words came out softly, timidly at first. Then with all the energy of his soul, he closed his eyes and lifted his face heavenward, singing the final phrase of the first verse—the only verse he knew. *The hopes and fears of all the years are met in thee tonight.*

Brandon stopped abruptly and took in the contrasting silence around him. And that's when he felt it. A tangible warmth rushed into him, as clearly as if a warm wind had come from nowhere to take his breath away. The peace he'd felt earlier suddenly magnified tenfold, consuming him with a perfect hope and serenity that he'd never imagined possible. He felt as if he could take on the world. He felt capable of overcoming any obstacle in his path. He felt completely void of pain. And that was the key. He knew he was capable and strong, because he knew he wasn't alone. He was at one with the Creator of heaven and earth, the Savior of the world; *his* Savior. He laughed through a rush of warm tears and basked in the reality of the sensation filling his heart and soul, then he put his hands on the keyboard—and he played. He played, he sang, he wept. Only through music could he fully express his joy. Only through this gift that God had given him could he articulate his gratitude to God.

He finished the song and sat quietly basking in the peace that echoed through the silence. He looked at his left hand; he opened and closed it, attempting to ease some of the stiffness. He felt angry with himself for not having done the therapy exercises, but he determined that he could start now, and he would do whatever it took to restore it to its full capacity. He simply wouldn't stand for anything less.

While Brandon sat there, another Christmas carol came to his mind, one of his favorites. "Hark the Herald Angels Sing." He picked it out with his right hand, then worked it into a lush embellishment that just seemed to flow right through him, as if the music came from a source outside himself, and he was merely the conduit with enough training and experience to make it happen. Again he used his left hand only enough to give it some depth with some repetitive low notes, while what he played with his right hand almost had the effect of an intricate music box.

Brandon was startled to catch movement in the room. He stopped playing and turned to see a couple of staff members standing in the room watching him, their expressions pleasant. A quick glance in the other direction told him the sun was coming up; the day was beginning.

"Oh, don't stop," one of them said. "It was beautiful. It would be nice to work to music for a change."

Brandon knew the regime here was strict, for employees as well as residents. He knew he wasn't where he was supposed to be, but he felt compelled to heed their request and said, "Well then, you'd better keep working, or they'll kick me out."

They both chuckled and began preparing the room for breakfast. Brandon was vaguely aware of the room slowly filling with people, mostly other patients. He just kept playing, trying not to let his audience distract him. He played the same two songs over and over, but nobody seemed to notice. He finally stopped, if only to try and ease the ache in his left hand. He was met with cheers and applause. He turned on the bench and chuckled, saying, "Sorry, I don't know many Christmas songs."

"Oh, there's some right here," a woman said, shooing him off the bench. She opened it and quickly produced a book of Christmas carols.

"So there is," Brandon said. He wasn't terribly fond of playing from a book, but taking a long glance at his small audience, he felt compelled to do so. He'd experienced endless hours of horrific group therapy with many of these people. Some of them had been on hard drugs for so long their brains were fried. He'd seen many of them break down and sob inconsolably; he'd heard many of them scream and swear and throw violent fits. Of course, he'd done all of this as well—but he'd managed to keep it corralled into his private sessions. But looking at these people now, they all looked mesmerized, perfectly calm, expectantly eager to hear him play something else. Breakfast was being served, but no one seemed interested in the food.

"Okay, well," he said, putting the book in front of him, "let's see what we can do. The left hand isn't working very well, but we'll give it a try."

He picked out the melody for "Away in a Manger," then when he had a feel for it he started over, making it more fluid. He played it twice, then moved on to "What Child Is This?"

The expected intrusion by a staff member came, urging everyone to eat breakfast while they had a chance. But Brandon kept playing and was relieved when no one told him he couldn't. He was asked by a couple of people if he was hungry and wanted to eat, but he politely declined. This was feeding him far better than whatever they were serving for breakfast. He was aware of people finishing their meal and then gathering around him again. Beginning to feel terribly conspicuous, Brandon said halfway through "Jingle Bells," "Okay guys, if you want me to keep playing, I think you need to sing. I'm not a one-man band, you know."

He got some chuckles, then a couple of brave voices began to sing, and the others gradually joined in. Brandon smiled and decided that maybe he *was* a one-man band. He'd never been able to make it in the music industry the way he'd always dreamed, but maybe that was okay. Maybe he'd simply misunderstood the gift he'd been given. Maybe he didn't have to make records and play in concerts to bless people's lives with the gift God had given him. He was making these people smile—and sing. He eased into playing "Silent Night," and he felt hard-pressed not to cry as he realized that a room full of dysfunctional drug addicts were singing about one of the greatest miracles that had ever occurred—the birth of the Savior of mankind. Did they feel the peace and the hope that he felt? Did they comprehend that what they were singing about was real? That it was the only thing capable of truly rescuing them from the pits they had dug themselves into?

When Brandon finished the song, he wasn't surprised to hear one of the assistant administrators say in a subtly harsh voice, "Okay, I think that's good. We all have job assignments or therapy sessions we should be in and—"

"That won't be necessary," a different voice said, and Brandon turned in the other direction to see *the* administrator of the place, sitting among the patients. In a gentle voice she added, "I think this is the best therapy we've *all* had in a long time." She motioned toward Brandon with her hand. "Please . . . go on. Let us know when you need a break."

"I'm fine," Brandon said.

"Play the one you were playing when we came in earlier," a gruff male voice said. "The really pretty one."

Brandon assumed he meant the one that had come out sounding like a music box. He began to play "Hark the Herald Angels Sing," which was far too intricate to sing along to, but they clearly enjoyed it. He moved into one song after another that they could sing, and he wondered why he'd not been able to play this way before now. He was using his left hand very little and managing fine. Perhaps it was because he'd always tried to play music that he'd already learned with both hands. And now he was playing music he'd not played for years, and in a completely different way. Some of it he'd never played before, so he had no predetermined notion of how it should sound.

It was nearly lunchtime before Brandon finally declared that he was exhausted. His left hand ached like it hadn't for months. But he got a standing ovation, and he got several hugs and handshakes as he moved away from the piano. After all the weeks he'd spent in this place, he'd suddenly made new friends. There would have been a time when he might have been irritated at people only liking him when they learned he had some talent. But he felt different now. He recognized that his gift gave him the ability and insight to reach beyond the normal barriers of human judgment and natural reactions.

The following day the administrator asked Brandon if he would be willing to play during lunch for the remaining days of his stay. He eagerly agreed. On the day before he was scheduled to leave, he looked out the window and watched the snow fall, smiling to himself as he anticipated going home—and being able to take this newfound peace with him.

Settling back into the routine at Lauren's home, Brandon felt a contentment within himself that he had not felt since his early childhood. He thoroughly enjoyed the Christmas preparations in a way he'd not been able to since his mother's death many years earlier. As they put up the Christmas tree, decorated the house, baked goodies, and made homemade candy, it almost felt like a dream.

That Christmas ended up being one of the best of Brandon's life. It was filled with warmth, and laughter, and gifts from the heart. But most importantly to Brandon, it was filled with music. When he first suggested that the family gather around the piano for some Christmas carols, his father and sister looked at him as if he'd lost his mind. They both cried as he made himself comfortable and began his newfound rendition of a Christmas classic, but within minutes they were singing along. The joy that he saw in the faces of his loved ones seemed to match the joy he felt within himself. Never had he imagined that he could find such delight in his ability to make music. Gathered around the piano with the family he'd come home to, singing Christmas carols and laughing, he knew he'd never felt so happy. A couple of times he glanced up at the painting of the Savior looking down upon them, and he silently thanked God for bringing him home.

About the Author

ANITA STANSFIELD has been writing for more than twenty years, and her best-selling novels have captivated and moved hundreds of thousands of readers with their deeply romantic stories and focus on important contemporary issues. Her interest in creating romantic fiction began in high school, and her work has appeared in national publications. *The Gift* is her twenty-seventh publication by Covenant.

Anita and her husband, Vince, are the parents of five children. They and their two cats live in Alpine, Utah. The author enjoys hearing from her readers and can be contacted at **info@anitastansfield.com**. She can also be reached by contacting Covenant at **www.covenant-lds.com**.